D0646709
WITHDRAWN
WINNIPEG
JAN 2 3 2013
PUBLIC LIBRARY

Penguin's Hidden Talent

by Alex Latimer

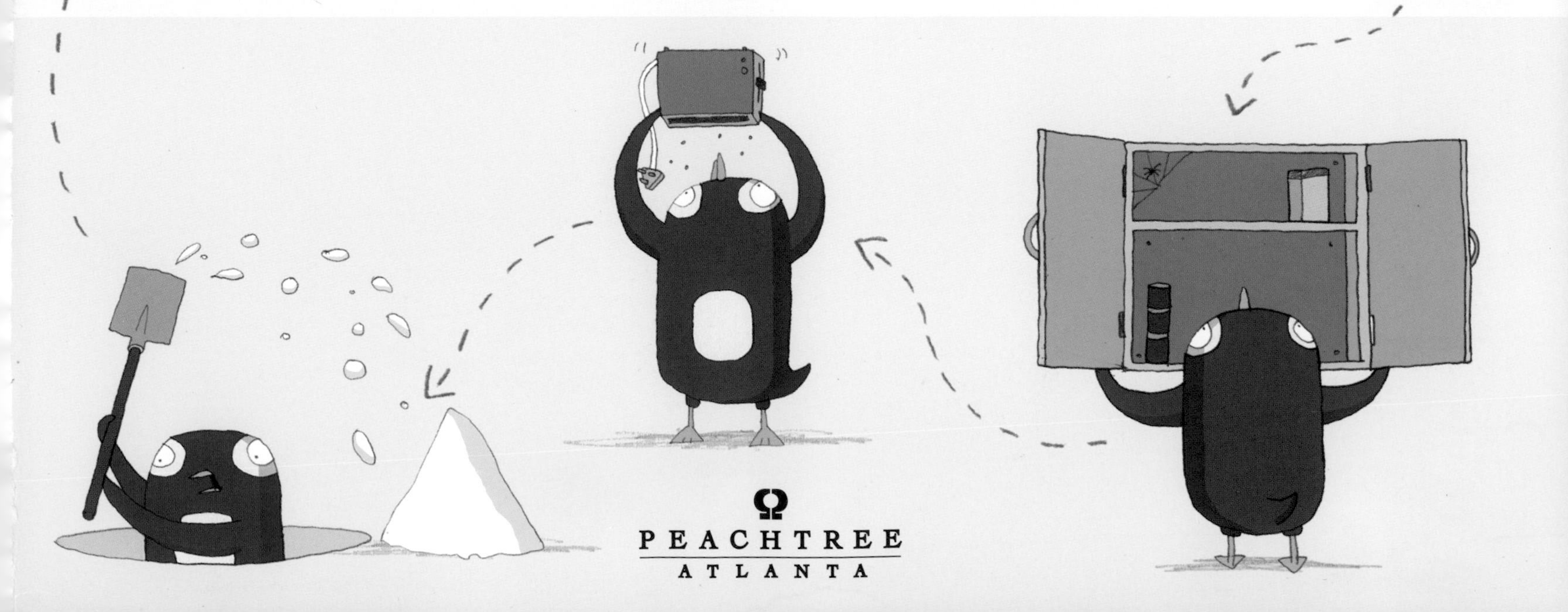

PEACHTREE
ATLANTA

Published by
PEACHTREE PUBLISHERS
1700 Chattahoochee Avenue
Atlanta, Georgia 30318-2112
www.peachtree-online.com

Originally published in Great Britain in 2012 by Random House.

Artwork created as pencil drawings, digitized, then finished with color and texture

10 9 8 7 6 5 4 3 2 1
First Edition

Library of Congress Cataloging-in-Publication Data

Latimer, Alex.
Penguin's hidden talent / written and Illustrated by Alex Latimer.
p. cm.
Summary: Penguin helps organize the annual talent show because he cannot identify his own gift, but when the show is over and the performers throw a party to show how much they appreciate Penguin's work, his aptitude becomes clear.
ISBN 978-1-56145-629-1 / 1-56145-629-2
[1. Ability--Fiction. 2. Talent shows--Fiction. 3. Penguins--Fiction. 4. Animals--Fiction.] I. Title.
aPZ7.L369612 Pen 2012
[E]--dc23
2011020996

Printed in February 2012 in China

The BIG annual Talent Show was
just around the corner. . .

. . .and everyone
was practicing.

Ta-da!

Everyone except Penguin.
Penguin couldn't figure out what his talent was.

It wasn't baking.

It wasn't map reading.

And it wasn't knitting.

Albatross wanted to help Penguin find his talent.
"Have you ever tried swallowing a whole marlin?" he asked.

But Penguin could only swallow a sardine.

Bear also wanted to help.
"Have you ever tried
juggling appliances?"
he asked.

But Penguin only managed to break a blender
and get a toaster stuck up a tree.

"Have you tried doing magic tricks?" asked Rabbit.
But though Penguin made Rabbit's watch disappear...

he couldn't bring it back again.

"Have you tried burping the alphabet?" asked Fox.

But all Penguin could do was hiccup.

"Don't worry about me," said Penguin. "I'll just help organize the Talent Show. That way I can still be involved, even though I don't have a talent."

So while his friends practiced
Penguin drew posters,

made phone calls,

sent e-mails,

and polished the trophy.

Finally the big day arrived.

The opening ceremony was terrific.

There were fireworks, and jets,
and lots of good music.

Then a guest speaker spoke.

And a famous band played.

Then the show started.

Albatross, Fox, Bear, and Rabbit all did exceptionally well.

kazam

The judges took forever to count up the points, but eventually they came to a decision.

With medals of excellence going to
Albatross, Fox, and Rabbit!"

Everyone celebrated.
But not Penguin.
After all, he didn't have a medal.

And he walked slowly home through the snow.

Bear, Albatross, Fox, and Rabbit were very worried about Penguin. They tried to think of a way to cheer him up.

"I know," said Rabbit.
"Let's throw Penguin a party
to thank him for organizing
the Talent Show!"

Everyone agreed that
it was a very good idea.

And they all
worked late
into the night
to organize a
great party.

The next morning, when Penguin came outside for the newspaper, he found that his friends had thrown him a party. And it wasn't a very good one.

Albatross had made a tattered banner
that said, THAKS PEMGIN.
The only music that Rabbit could organize
was a singing canary.
Fox brought his grandma as the guest speaker.
And Bear brought an old loaf of bread
instead of a cake.

"If only you'd organized this party, Penguin," said Rabbit. "Then it wouldn't be so terrible."

And just then, Penguin realized how talented he really was.

Hello. I'd like to order. . .

ice cream
What a great party!

Penguin Rocks
What a great talent!

PENGUIN
PARTY PLANNER
CALL: LOUDLY